Community Unit School
Dist. #11
Jr. H.S. Library
Hoopeston, Illinois

MW01153382

DISCARD

796.81
Gce

CHRISTOPHER J. GOEDECKE
ROSMARIE HAUSHERR

The WIND WARRIOR

The Training of a Karate Champion

Four Winds Press ✳ *New York*

Maxwell Macmillan Canada   Toronto
Maxwell Macmillan International
New York   Oxford   Singapore   Sydney

**Community Unit School
Dist. #11
Jr. H.S. Library
Hoopeston, Illinois**

12,630

*This book is dedicated to the wind that
fans our dreams, and to the warrior
within us all who strives for peace and
harmony in the spirit of Karate-Dō*
—C. G.

*Text copyright © 1992 by Christopher J. Goedecke. Illustrations copyright © 1992
by Rosmarie Hausherr. All rights reserved. No part of this book may be reproduced
or transmitted in any form or by any means, electronic or mechanical, including
photocopying, recording, or by any information storage and retrieval system, without permission in writing from the Publisher. Four Winds Press, Macmillan Publishing Company. 866 Third Avenue, New York, NY 10022 Maxwell Macmillan
Canada, Inc., 1200 Eglinton Avenue East, Suite 200, Don Mills, Ontario M3C
3N1. Macmillan Publishing Company is part of the Maxwell Communication
Group of Companies. Printed and bound in the United States of America.*
10 9 8 7 6 5 4 3 2

*The text of this book is set in Palatino.   Book design by Christy Hale
Library of Congress Cataloging-in-Publication Data   Goedecke, Christopher J.
The wind warrior : the training of a Karate champion / by Christopher J.
Goedecke : photographs by Rosmarie Hausherr.—1st ed.   p.   cm. Sum-
mary: Describes, in text and black-and-white photographs, the training of a thirteen-
year-old boy for a karate competition.   ISBN 0–02–736262–0.   1. Karate for
children—Juvenile literature. 2. Karate for children—Training—Juvenile
literature. [1. Karate.] I. Hausherr, Rosmarie, ill.   II. Title.
GV1114.32.G64 1992   796.8'153'083—dc20   91-6405*

*This book is not intended as a substitute for professional advice or
guidance in the field of the martial arts, nor is this book intended
to be used as a martial arts manual. A young person should take
part in the activities discussed and/or pictured in this book only
under the supervision of a knowledgeable and trained adult.*

Acknowledgments

Taking the photographs for The Wind Warrior *was a challenging
experience, yet thanks to Nicholas Armitage it was also a pleasant
one. In true karate spirit, Nick put his best effort into the physically
demanding photo sessions. The support from Nick's families and
friends was also a valuable asset. A big thank you to all of Christopher Goedecke's karate students for their enthusiastic participation. I am also grateful to the management of the Madison YMCA,
the Chatham Racket Club, and Eosin Panther Supplies for allowing
me to photograph on their premises. Professional assistance was
generously offered by Mel Klein, Director of the New Jersey State
Karate Games Tournament. Thanks to all the tournament judges
and officials for their cooperation. I am thankful to my photographer
colleague, Felix Wey, who collaborated with me at the New Jersey
State Karate Games Tournament. His photographs appear on pages
47, 48, 51, 55, 60, and 63.*

*The chikara on the back of the jacket was created by Shiman Eido
Roshi, Abbot of the Zen Studies Society, a parent organization of
Dai Bosatsu Zendo Kondo-Ji.*

Contents

Meet Nick

"Hai yaaa!" shouts the hero of a Saturday-afternoon karate movie as he thrashes several black-hooded ninja villains. In their family living room, two brothers sit glued to the TV. When a commercial comes on they launch into a replay of the fight: hands chop, legs snap, bodies bend and twist, and fists jab the air.

Nick Armitage knows the right moves to make now when one of his older brothers roughhouses with him. He's come a long way since the days when he sat, as a six-year-old, on the sidelines watching Peter and Alex advance through the colored-belt ranks of karate.

At thirteen, Nicholas Dillon Armitage is five feet two inches and ninety-five pounds. He is a seasoned *karate-ka* (student). He attends karate classes in his hometown of Madison, New Jersey, practicing in both the children's and adults' programs. Occasionally, he even helps his teacher instruct younger members.

Nick has grown half a foot taller and forty-four pounds heavier since the day he joined the Madison YMCA karate club after his seventh birthday. Seven was the minimum age for enrollment.

Nick now has six years of karate training under his dark brown belt. The coveted black belt—the sign of an expert—is three promotions away.

Nick likes challenges. In four months he is going to enter a karate tournament, New Jersey's biggest state-run karate competition. He will test his martial arts skills in the advanced boys' division, competing in two events: sparring and forms. During the spring and into early summer he will train hard with other students, on his own, and under the watchful eye of his instructor, a karate master, to sharpen his fighting techniques in the drive to become both a black belt expert and a champion. This is his story.

Off to the Dojo!

It's Saturday morning. Out late at the movies with his friends the night before, Nick does not wake up until eleven o'clock.

Nick lives with his mom and his stepfather, Dennis, his two brothers, and his fifteen-year-old stepsister, Jackie. Nick's mom, Georganna, and dad, Norman, were divorced when Nick was eight. Both his parents remarried. Luckily, they live in the same town, so Nick spends time with each of them.

At breakfast he eats three big bowls of cereal. Then he rolls the jacket and pants of his uniform together, lashes his belt around them, and slings the neat pack over his neck. He calls good-bye to his mother; then he's out the door and off to the

dojo at the Y. *Dojo*, which means "way place," is the name given to a karate practice area. At the Y's rear entrance he meets his friend Henry McCann, another brown belt. "Sorry, Nick, I can't be at class today," he says.

The downstairs desk attendant hands Nick a locker key. In the boys' locker room, he changes into his karate uniform, or *gi*. Nick loops his brown *obi*, or belt, twice around his waist and finishes with a square knot.

Students assemble in the spacious new gymnastics center a few minutes before the 1:30 practice begins. Saturday's classes are held here by special arrangement. *Sensei*, the teacher, likes to use the center's special spring-matted floor.

Nick helps Samantha tie her *gi* jacket and *obi*. The design of the *gi* has not changed much from the simple clothing worn by the farmers and fishermen of Okinawa, Japan, hundreds of years ago. It is loose-fitting, so the body can move freely. There are no zippers or buttons. Everything is tied with cloth strings. Sensei teaches that the first sign of self-respect is a neat, clean appearance.

"Line up!" Sensei shouts.

Students line up according to belt rank. The darker the belt, the higher the rank.

Most karate schools follow the *kyu-dan* system of grading. This consists of colored belt ranks from eighth to first *kyu* (class). Nick is a *sankyu* (third-class brown). In Nick's school, the belt progression is white (*hachikyu* or eighth *kyu*), yellow, orange, blue, green, and three levels of brown.

Next follow the *dan* grades. There are ten degrees of black belt, each called a *dan*. *Shodan* is first-degree black.

Nick is the senior student. He takes his position on the front line to Sensei's right. Then he turns toward the class and yells, "*Kyotsuke!*" ("Ready?")

Thirty-eight young *gi*-clad boys and girls from ages six to fourteen and the four adult assistants respond in unison: "*Hai.*" ("Yes.")

"*Seiza!*" Sensei commands.

Students kneel in the formal Japanese seated posture called *seiza*, back straight, hands on knees with feet crossed. They are taught that an alert mind is prepared for anything.

Nick's teacher is a master of *isshinryu*, the "one heart" method. It is a popular Okinawan karate style in New Jersey. Sensei has been studying karate for twenty-four years. He is six feet four inches tall. He towers above the young students. Hundreds of children come to learn from him.

Sensei checks attendance from his class roster. Each student answers "*Hai!*" after his or her name is called.

"*Rei!*" ("Bow.") Bodies lower respectfully into the bow. Every class begins and ends with this formal ritual. Sensei says bowing is like shaking hands, Japanese style. It is also a sign of trust. In ancient Japan, lowering your head showed that you trusted a person not to cut it off with a sword!

When Sensei began training in 1968, nearly all the commands were in Japanese. Today many American karate teachers mix traditional Japanese rituals with English commands, but Sensei believes that the Japanese commands give the art a special flavor.

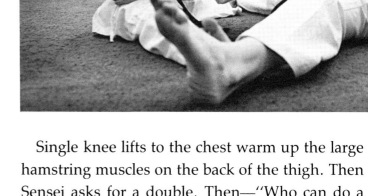

"Let's begin! Who can jump up from *seiza* without using hands?" he asks.

Nick pops right up. His legs are strong. Some of the others have trouble with the challenge, but they give it their best try.

Warm-ups follow. Leg stretching and strengthening is first. Their teacher tells them, "If you try to mold cold clay, it will break into pieces. But if you warm it up you can shape it easily. Muscles are like clay. Warming them up properly lets them stretch easily."

Two-person stretches really loosen you up. "Be careful," Sensei reminds them. "Don't pull too hard. He's not a wishbone!"

Single knee lifts to the chest warm up the large hamstring muscles on the back of the thigh. Then Sensei asks for a double. Then—"Who can do a triple?"

He demonstrates a triple knee lift to the chest. Only Nick and a few other students can do it. Several fall down on the soft mat trying to lift their knees alternately three times before landing.

Next the class drills basic techniques. Upper body strikes first: straight punch . . . palm heel . . . spear hand . . . back fist . . . knife hand . . . elbow. Each strike is repeated twenty times. Kicking drills follow: front snap kick . . . back kick . . . side kick . . . knee strike . . . squat kick. Then they drill blocks: low block . . . middle block . . . high block.

Good karate demonstrates self-defense, not an offensive self. Blocks can deter a bully from fighting. So defense is stressed, although some blocks can even break an attacker's arm.

"Faster, harder!" Sensei counts out in Japanese: "*Ichi* (one), *ni* (two), *san* (three), *shi* (four) . . ." Nick is used to the counting. He barks the numbers back. The sound of the counting cadence fills the center.

"Roundhouse kick from a T stance!" Nick spreads his legs wide, making the shape of the letter T. His whole body must torque, or twist, to give power to the kick, which can surprise an opponent by sneaking around his guard. Glenn ducks out of the way of Nick's roundhouse during a two-person drill.

Students strike the air to learn body control. But karate is not just kicking or punching empty space. So next, everyone lines up to kick the green foam striking shields. "Make sure to hold the pads properly!" they are instructed. "Stay in a strong stance!"

Wham! Tony feels the kick's power through the shield.

Sensei brings out a special electronic striking pad that can measure a kick's impact. Scoring a twenty-five is equivalent to one hundred pounds of force.

An assistant holds the pad. Everyone gets a turn. The first student tries a front kick, and Sensei reads aloud from the hand-held electronic box. "Forty-three! Side kick, thirty-seven!"

Several younger students try back kicks. One boy attempts a flying knee strike. "Fifty-two! Very good," Sensei says. Patrick hits a nine, just below his age of ten. Christine scores fifty-four. John scores a sixty-two with a flying front kick.

It's Nick's turn. He runs across the floor, leaps up, and connects with a solid flying side kick. "Eighty-five!" Sensei announces. "That's three hundred and forty pounds of force!"

"Whoa!" the class exclaims.

Next the students pair up for light sparring, a free-fighting exercise. Strikes thrown may not touch your partner's body. Blocking is the only contact allowed.

Nick coaches two seven-year-old yellow belts, Jon-Paul and Gregory, calling out pointers. "Keep your guards up! Use more kicks! Jon-Paul, keep your hands closed."

Sensei watches a different sparring pair. Uh-oh! Ryan lost control, and Joseph got kicked. Sensei has the two boys sit face-to-face. Ryan apologizes. Joseph accepts. The rule on the mat is "All those who come in as friends should leave as friends."

Close call: A round kick taps Deanna's cheek. She's okay—just surprised. Deanna trains with her two brothers, Cooper and Tony.

"Line up!" Sensei calls. Nick asks if everyone is ready to end.

"*Hai*" ("yes") they shout.

"*Rei.*" Class is over.

Nick stops at the water fountain.

"Hey, watch out!" he says, playfully spraying Christine and her brother, David.

Favorite Sports

Karate is Nick's main sport and the most important thing in his life right now. But he also enjoys other activities.

To build up strength, he lifts weights. He has a bench and free weights in the basement, which doubles as Peter's room. Peter helped Nick make up a weight-lifting routine.

"My strength has definitely increased," Nick says. He bench presses and curls with moderately heavy weights.

In the winter, when snow conditions are good, his dad takes him skiing in Vermont or upstate New York just about every weekend.

Nick also Rollerblades with friends in a newly paved parking lot near his home. He hopes to join the Madison High School hockey team as a freshman next year. So he and Alex practice hockey in the driveway to ready him for the fall tryouts. Peter, an avid cyclist, watches.

After house chores, Nick finishes his workout indoors with a few rounds against George, his eighty-pound punching bag.

Eight Against One: Kata with the Adults

It's a rainy Wednesday evening. Georganna, Nick's mom, drives him to the adult class at the Chatham *dojo* a few miles from the Y. Nick is here to fine-tune his *kata*.

Karate students practice special patterns of movements called katas, or forms. Nick must learn nine of these traditional exercises to advance to the black belt.

Tonight's class will train on the kata *seiuchin* (say-u-chin). This is the deep horse-stance kata. A horse stance is a straddle-legged posture that strengthens the lower body. Class members view their movements in full-length mirrors covering the front wall of Studio A.

"Seiuchin is an excellent tournament kata," Sensei says, "because the form is very strong!"

Nick is used for an example of good kata. "Form should be pleasing to the eye, like a dancer's posture," Sensei tells them. "It must have dynamic lines." He holds a stick in front of Nick's body. "See how his arms and legs form the shape of an X? But if one arm bends too much, this X will look crooked. The form will look sloppy. Power flows through a properly positioned body.

"You must pay attention to even the smallest moves," the teacher continues. "The difference between a good karate-ka and a great karate-ka is attention to detail. Thank you, Nick."

Try holding a deep horse stance for five minutes. Phew!

Sensei reveals a leg-sweep takedown hidden in *seiuchin*. Takedowns are moves to make an opponent fall.

"Pair up and practice this leg sweep," Sensei directs them. "The more you repeat a fighting technique, the better it gets. Throwing a ball once, even a hundred times, does not make a great pitcher." Sensei's first teacher told him a karate technique is not your own until you have done it at least ten thousand times!

Nick throws Andrea, a female black belt. In another drill he is paired with Ivan. A butcher by trade, Ivan grabs Nick like a piece of meat and sends a lightning-fast spear hand one inch away from his solar plexus, a lethal pressure point below the chest.

Community Unit Sch...
Dist. #11
Jr. H.S. Library
Hoopeston, Illinois

Katas are the dictionary of fighting moves. They were created by Asian masters as a simple way of passing on their personal fighting secrets. Many are several hundred years old. Each kata has a name. The first one, called *seisan* (pronounced "say-san"), is the oldest kata taught on Okinawa. A kata is made up of sixty to a hundred movements that are performed with painstaking precision. A single kata takes only minutes to perform but months to learn and years to master.

Katas are not exotic dances. There are lethal fighting techniques hidden in these beautiful forms. For example, in the *kusanku* kata, Nick fights eight imaginary opponents.

According to traditional Japanese masters, form is the essence of good karate. When one studies kata, he or she is studying form. Kata training develops power, beauty, discipline, and inner strength. It builds coordination and mental concentration, and increases endurance, timing, control, and speed.

Kata is probably the most difficult thing for young karate-ka to learn, since they have to memorize hundreds of movements in a precise pattern right down to the bend in the toes. Sensei says, "Young people who only want to practice fighting miss a real challenge in kata study."

Kusanku kata was named after a Chinese diplomat known for his great jumping ability. *Kusanku* is demanding, with its jumps and one-leg drops. Nick wants to perform this kata at the games.

"Turn your body a little more to the right," Sensei advises him. "Align your right arm with your right leg. There, good! Okay, let's continue. X-block . . . middle block . . . punch . . . punch . . . turn . . . back fist . . . jump!"

While airborne, Nick slaps his foot with the bottom of his hand and then drops low to the ground.

At 9:30 the formal class ends. Georganna waits in the corridor to take Nick home as her son receives final kata pointers from his teacher.

"Keep your chin up and shoulders back. It shows confidence in the movement!"

"Okay," Nick says.

Karate—from East to West

Nick is one of thousands of young American students practicing the Japanese art of karate.

Karate is a martial art. The English word *martial* derives from Mars, the Roman god of war. The martial arts include dozens of popular Asian unarmed fighting methods such as Korean tae kwon do, or Chinese kung fu wu shu. But the largest number of martial arts comes from Japan, from the rich military culture of the legendary *bushi* or *samurai* warrior. From the early 1600s, when the reign of the last shogun family to rule Japan began, until 1868, when ruling power was restored to the emperor, Japan was dominated by intense warfare and civil strife. Over this violent period the military tradition and the warrior arts reached a high level of importance and influenced the entire Japanese population.

Of all the great Japanese martial arts, such as judo, jujitsu, sumo, aikido, and kendo, karate is the most popular in the world. You can find *dojos* around the globe. In the United States alone there are an estimated 5,400 karate schools, clubs, and courses. Karate's history in the United States, though, is young. It began in the 1950s when some American soldiers stationed in Japan and Okinawa returned to the States after World War II

with a powerful fighting art that used every part of the body as a lethal weapon.

They put on public demonstrations, splintering stacks of pine, crushing roofing tiles with jackhammer fist blows, finger-poking bricks in half, and dispelling hordes of would-be attackers with a tiger's speed. Such shows sparked tremendous curiosity and popularized the idea that superhuman skills were not just for the superheroes. By the 1970s young and old packed the karate schools and clubs that had sprung up across America.

Karate's history began on the tiny island called Okinawa during the fourteenth century. Okinawa is the largest of the Ryukyu Islands, a chain south of the Japanese mainland. The Okinawans developed their art to defend themselves against the oppressive rule of Japanese overlords. They referred to their unarmed methods as *te* (hand). This simple name helped to keep it secret. Later they combined the name with the ideogram *kara* to form *kara-te* ("China hand"). An ideogram is a written symbol that expresses an idea; China was once known as the *"kara"* kingdom. The word was added to show respect for the Chinese influence on fighting techniques.

In 1921 a scholarly Okinawan martial arts teacher named Gichin Funakoshi demonstrated his amazing "new" fighting art to the crown prince of Japan, who was later to become the emperor Hirohito. Funakoshi had taken up karate as an eleven-year-old boy to overcome his frail physique. The crown prince was so impressed with Funakoshi's powerful demonstration that Japanese schools began to include instruction in the *kara-te* art. They also modernized the "China" ideogram to its present day usage: *kara-te*, the "empty-hand" art. Funakoshi's teaching and demonstration heralded the spread of karate throughout the world.

The Tournament Application Arrives

The tournament application arrives on a Saturday. Nick's dad, Norman, helps him to fill out the entry form. "The tournament is on Sunday, July 8, at the Middlesex Vo-Tech High School in East Brunswick," Norman reads.

Nick checks off the forms and sparring events. Good news! The age range in the advanced boys' division is twelve to fourteen years old. Nick will be the oldest in his division. He turned fourteen in May.

Nick removes twenty-two dollars from a metal cashbox in his room to pay for the entry fee. He gives it to his dad in exchange for a check to be mailed.

Snap! A back fist cuts the air as Nick imagines he's sparring at the tournament.

Later he reads a story to his other stepsister, five-year-old Alexandra.

"Come on, Nick, I'll drive you to class," his dad says.

Gear Up for Sparring!

Fifty students turn out for a two-hour sparring workshop in the Y's gymnastics center. The soft floor is ideal for *jiu-kumite* (free-sparring). Free-sparring is not actual fighting; one helps to teach, the other just hurts. Students must learn the difference.

The tournament is only five weeks away. It's time to brush up on fighting skills. Black belts Joe and Andrea, along with Henry McCann, are here to assist Sensei.

The class lines up and bows. Sensei announces, ''We're going to run three rings. Six- to eight-year-olds with Mr. McCann. Nine- to eleven-year-olds in the corner with Mr. Noonan. Twelve and up, in the center with me.'' Using chairs and pads as corner markers, volunteers set up three twenty-by-twenty-foot areas.

Class member Jeff dumps two large plastic bags filled with sparring equipment onto the floor. He pairs up sets of leather gloves and foam boots. The fighters wear protective padding to minimize injury.

Sensei tells the instructors, ''Make sure everyone gets a chance to fight.''

Henry's group is the largest. In one match Joshua chases Brett around the floor. *Pop!* A snap punch bounces off the tip of Brett's nose.

Crack . . . swish . . . thump . . . smack! Two spirited blue belts collide in Joe Noonan's ring. He steps in between to calm the two boys.

In the center ring Nick watches Paul and Mat hurling head-high kicks at each other.

After dozens of matches, one large ring is created for some judged sparring.

Sensei talks about the general rules of tournament competition. "Tournament karate is not the same as real fighting," he tells the class. "Only punches and kicks are used. Other karate techniques are illegal in competition. They are only for self-defense." Matthew and Nick demonstrate a forbidden groin kick and ankle twist.

While all types of tournaments allow powerful blocks, the rules vary according to how hard you can strike. There are actually three general kinds of sparring matches: full contact, where you can hit as hard as you want; semicontact, where medium to light torso contact is allowed; and non-contact, where only light body contact is allowed. Light contact is striking about as hard as clapping your hands. The Garden State Games is a semicontact tournament.

Sensei sets up the traditional judging system by choosing four corner judges. Sensei will referee, moving closely in the ring with the fighters. When the referee sees a strike delivered by a competitor, he or she will stop the match and ask the corner judges to make a decision about its effectiveness. Each corner judge can vote that one, one-half, or no point be awarded. A fighter will score for a strike if he or she gets a total of at least two and a half points from the judges.

Sensei acquaints the class with the judges' hand signals: one finger means the judge votes the fighter should get one point, a fist means a half point, lowered hands means no point, hands over eyes means the judge did not see it, and hands rolling means too much happening! A hand chopping arm means illegal contact. Two fists clashing means that both fighters struck blows at the same time, so no point is given.

A fighter is disqualified if more than two judges call contact.

"Nick and Mat, you're up first!" The boys bow to their teacher, then each other, showing that this is a match of strength and skill without the intent to hurt. Full-force blows must stop one to three inches from your opponent.

"Cross hands," Sensei says. *"Hajime!"* ("Begin!") The two probe with jabs and short kicks. Swish, snap! Nick sneaks a straight punch under Mat's ribs.

"Yame!" ("Stop!") Sensei yells. He reenacts Nick's punch for the class and turns to the judges. "Jeff?" He did not see it. "Henry?" Half point. "Joe?" One point. "Jack?" No point. "No score!" Sensei tells the fighters.

"Continue!" he shouts. Now Mat attacks with a face-high round kick. He scores one point.

A back kick and round kick give Nick a 2–1 victory.

"Next fighters up." Two others waiting on the sidelines move into the ring.

Nick spars with everyone differently. "I do lots of high-low attacks," he says. "At orange belt I learned to fake high and attack low or vice versa. I also like to use lots of distractions, then come in with a fast lunge punch." The punch works twice in a match with green belt Veronika. But Veronika is good at charging and jamming Nick's kicks.

Nick and Henry are called to spar. Henry charges, narrowly missing Nick with a front kick but landing a fast back kick to his midsection. In another clash, Nick slips and falls to the ground. "Henry doesn't always defend his body well enough," Nick says. Nick knows Henry's weak points because they often spar together.

Nick catches him off guard with a front kick under the arm. He surprises the lower belts by beating Henry, 3–2.

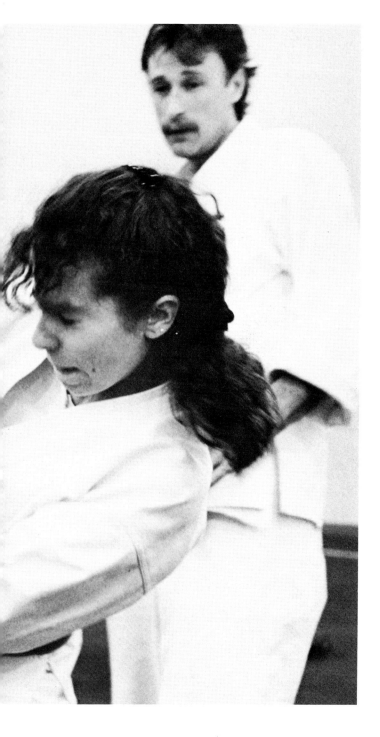

A little comedy breaks the tension of the sparring matches when a young blue-belted student named Richard is chosen to spar Henry. Richard is so nervous about sparring a brown belt he decides it's better to just drop dead on the floor rather then trade punches. Everyone gets a good laugh. Henry gets a new partner.

By the end of the day, Nick is a tired victor. He talks in the locker room with Henry and Kevin about their favorite techniques.

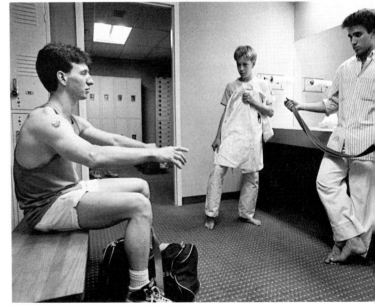

At the Chiropractor's

Karate practice presents some personal challenges for Nick. He remembers being a first grader and waking up crying one morning with his right side in excruciating pain. The family doctor diagnosed his problem as a condition called Legg-Perthes. It is a deformation of the "ball" in the ball-and-socket joint of the hip. It causes Nick's hips to be unstable.

Nick spent two weeks on crutches. His doctor told him his body might outgrow the problem within two years, but the symptoms have only lessened in the past year. Side kicks and back kicks aggravate the Legge-Perthes.

A visit to Dr. Larry Bakur's chiropractic office once every three weeks seems to help. After checking the alignment of Nick's legs, Larry makes several adjustments in his patient's lower spine and neck to realign the pelvis. Five minutes later, Nick is finished.

"That feels better," Nick tells him. Sometimes the Legge-Perthes gets so bad he cannot kick at all.

Wood and Steel

The sun burns brightly in the late afternoon over the Madison High School field. A handful of "upper" belts are synchronizing their movements with the long *bo* (staff) during an outdoor weapons class. Footwork is hidden for those wearing the black-skirted *hakama*.

"Turn and thrust," Sensei calls out. Nick lunges forward, repeating a movement possibly used once by some Okinawan warrior to knock his opponent off a horse. Nick made his long *bo* from a pine dowel he bought at the hardware store.

Long *bo* sparring! The six-foot stick goes whooshing over Nick's head. Nobody wants to get too close to the action of those giant chopsticks. Nick pokes at Andrea's body. She swats the end of his *bo* away and tries to bang his fingers.

Kobudo, or weapons arts, are taught only to advanced students.

When the Japanese took over Okinawa, they confiscated the people's weapons. For self-protection, the Okinawans instead turned their tools of labor into weapons. They made lethal use of the wooden sticks called *nunchaku*; the *tonfa*, a wooden device used by many police today; the long *bo*; and the sickle-shaped *kama*. Advanced

modern karate students continue to carry on the tradition of those skills.

"A famous Japanese swordsman was once defeated by a stick. Common objects within your reach often make the best weapons," Sensei says.

The specialty of Nick's school is the short *bo* called the *hanbo*, a three-foot hardwood ministaff. "It's probably the only practical weapon today," Sensei comments. "Look around you; a cane, umbrella, bat, broom, mop, stick, or tree branch will suffice."

They all form a circle for the *bo* toss. With one hand behind their backs, they quickly toss a single *hanbo* around the ring. A second *bo* is added. Then three at a time. Nick tries to keep up the pace and not lose concentration.

The short *bo* is practical, fast, and easily carried. Andrea shows the group how to use it to immobilize Tom in a pretzel-like lock.

Nunchaku are lightning fast. The free-twirling end is almost invisible and very unpredictable. "Chux," as some people call them, can also be used as handcuffs by twisting the cord around a wrist.

Under Sensei's supervision Nick wields two steel *sai* to practice the *kusanku sai* kata. Long ago, three were carried and one was used for throwing. The two points of a *sai*, called tines, can lock the blade of a sword. Arms tire easily holding the heavy steel weapons.

Two curved blades called *kama* in Sensei's hands slice the air. *Kama* are dangerous. The sharp blades can injure the user as easily as they might a would-be assailant. Therefore, Sensei only allows advanced adult students to practice with them.

Karate weapons are not toys. Although they can teach the user advanced principles of self-defense, they are tools of destruction and should be handled with the utmost care. Many states ban the sale of most martial arts weapons to minors, and most karate instructors will only allow skilled students to practice with them under supervision.

New Gloves and New Gi

Tournament judges like to see neat-looking competitors. Since first impressions are important, Nick decides to buy a pair of sparring gloves and a new *gi* for the tournament.

Henry McCann offers to drive him to the supply store in Clifton, New Jersey. Eosin Panther is a family martial arts supply store. The owner and his wife say they operate the only mom-and-pop store in the country that exclusively sells martial arts equipment. It's run by Edward O. Noll and his Korean wife, Soon Ie, who named the store for their initials. They have been in the business sixteen years. Soon Ie designs karate uniforms. Of their five children, two boys are black belts.

Their store carries all kinds of specialized equipment: weapons, uniforms, books, videos, punching bags, patches. Area instructors come in to chat about business and their upcoming events.

Nick looks at a good-quality heavy-weight 100-percent cotton uniform: seventy-four dollars. He hopes he has enough money saved from his ten-dollar-a-month allowance.

Uniform sizes go from 0 to 6. Nick tries on a size 3. It fits fine, with a little room to grow.

"How about this all-American *gi*?" Ed asks.

"They'd really notice you in the tournament in that one," Henry says.

School's Out!

Nick jokes around on the last day of school with Ted, Joshua, Ben, and Mat. He has lots of friends.

Nick had a good year in school. He's an A-B student. Math and science are his favorite subjects. Some people know he does karate. "But," he says, "if anyone starts bothering me, I know my limits. If the kid's bigger, I talk my way out of it."

Nick the Competitor

In 1982, New Jersey created a series of thirty sporting events for the state's amateur athletes, similar to the world Olympic Games. Events range from cycling to volleyball. Unlike the other sports, the karate eliminations and finals are both held in one day over an eleven-hour period. It's the largest participation event of the entire games' showcase as well as Sensei's biggest school rally.

Nick first competed at the Garden State Games tournament the previous summer. He won two medals.

Most competitors do not win the first time; many never win. This Sunday will be his second attempt at competition.

Nick is part of his karate school's team of forty competitors: thirty-four males and six females. The youngest is Mark, age six. The oldest is Steve, age thirty-nine.

One of the symbols of Nick's school is Fujin, the god of the wind in Japanese mythology. Japanese legend tells of Fujin running through the sky, catching the wind in his sack and stirring it up. Sensei says his devoted students are like Fujin: they have lots of energy. So he calls his team the Wind Warriors.

Off to the Tournament!

It's 8:15 A.M.! Nick's alarm failed to go off at 7:30. He bolts out of bed and dresses quickly as Henry honks his horn outside. He runs out the door with a bagel sticking out of his mouth and two clutched in his hand. The car zooms south.

The Games Begin

Cool, cloudy weather dispels fears of a sweltering day for the tournament. A steady stream of spectators and competitors spill out of their cars into the Middlesex Vo-Tech parking lot. Dozens of athletes gather, waiting to register.

"Spectators around front. Athletes through here," the official at the side door announces.

Nick and Henry arrive at 9:30, unpack the car, then go inside to sign in. Anxious Wind Warriors group in a corner of the gym. The room bustles with people.

"Are you nervous, Nick?" Sensei asks.

"I'm more excited than nervous," he answers.

Four hundred amateur karate athletes fill the north side bleachers. It is a record turnout: 220 children and 180 adults. Sensei gives instructions to his assistants. Then he gathers the students for a pep talk.

"There are six numbered rings on the floor. Listen carefully for your ring assignments. If anyone has any problems or questions let me know. . . . Jeff is in charge of equipment. . . ." He explains the sparring rules while another assistant ties children's *obi*. Nick and his dad perch in the bleachers, watching the crowd.

At 10:30 A.M. the games get under way.

"All rise for our national anthem," the tournament director, Mel Klein, says over the mike. After "The Star-Spangled Banner" he announces, "We are going to begin with children's forms."

The noise level in the gym makes it impossible to hear the ring assignments. Sensei sends Ben to the official's table to write down who goes where.

Forms

Six-year-old Wind Warriors Mark and Michael are instructed to go immediately to Ring 1.

"Mark Susko?" an official reads from a card. Mark approaches the five seated judges. After a crisp bow, he says, "My name is Mark Susko. I am going to do *seisan* kata." He bows again, then steps backward to a taped spot on the floor. With a nod from the judges, Mark begins his form as the crowd watches. This is his first tournament. A little nervous, he forgets some moves and starts over. The judges hold up their scorecards.

In another ring twenty-seven boys and girls patiently sit awaiting their turn to perform. The Wind Warriors cheer when Veronika captures a first-place gold for *chinto* kata.

Seventeen-year-old Henry McCann *kiais* loudly during his kata performance. The *kiai* adds power to the movements. Henry has been a kata winner for the last five years at the games, but this is his first year competing in the adult division.

Three Wind Warriors are called up. "Kevin Smith, honorable mention; Phil Ott, third place; Henry McCann . . . first place."

"Yay!" Everyone applauds. Sensei is smiling.

"Boys' advanced red- and brown-belt forms—Ring 3!"

"You're up, Nick," a student informs him. Nick goes to the far corner ring and speaks with the other boys while he waits. Nick is the fourth boy to compete.

"My name is Nick Armitage," he tells the judges. "I am going to perform *kusanku* kata." He bows crisply. Then he snaps sharply through his opening moves: block . . . punch . . . punch . . . turn . . . kick . . . jump!

Many competitors start strong but end weak.
Nick remembers Sensei's kata advice in the adult
class. He finishes and bows.

Scorecards are lifted: 6.7, 6.7, 7.3, 7.4, 7.2. High and low scores are dropped, so Nick leads the competition with a 21.2 out of a possible 30.

After the last boy has gone, Nick feels confident his kata was one of the best.

A judge steps forward. Another approaches with the medals.

The first judge says, "Winner of the third place, bronze medal, Kitab Ismail. Second place, silver medal, Jeffrey Ariola. First place, gold medal, Nick Armitage."

Applause rings out from Wind Warriors, friends, family, and other spectators scattered throughout the gym.

"Go to the cafeteria area for picture-taking," an official tells them. The three happy victors retreat through a side exit.

Georganna and Norman congratulate their son, beaming.

Competitive Sparring

Veronika's earlier victory in kata is offset by her shocking defeat during her first experience at tournament sparring. In less than one minute she is bested by her aggressive competitor, 2–0.

"The match happened so fast it was a blur. I was angry that I could not do more," she said later. She wanted another chance. However, having lost her first match, she was now out of the sparring competition.

"Twelve- to fourteen-year-old red and brown belts, Ring 2," the announcer says. That's Nick's sparring group. Ringside, Sensei checks his gear and gives him pointers. One boy who studies *goju* karate confides to Nick that he's pretty nervous. Another recognizes Nick from the kata division.

"Nick Armitage and Joseph Gangemi," a ref calls. They step into the ring. A red cloth strip is looped through Nick's belt; he is the red fighter. With their protective headgear, both boys look like weird vinyl insects. Nick sizes up his opponent. He has been taught to use his height as an advantage against a shorter person by using a lot of kicks.

"Begin!" the referee shouts. Nick jumps forward and lands a solid back kick. His opponent tumbles out of the ring but springs back with plenty of fighting spirit.

Four red flags rise. "One point for the red fighter." The kick hurt Nick's hip. It begins to throb.

Nick attacks strongly with a flurry of body punches and scores the winning point.

After a short rest Nick must challenge a boy named David who is clearly a head taller. David won his first match using kicks.

Nick's strategy is to close in quickly with punches. However, when the match begins, the tall boy scores a direct kick to Nick's stomach. It hurts. One point for David!

This is where having two big brothers helps. Nick charges and throws a body punch. One point!

After several more clashes, Nick scores a front kick to David's midsection for a 2–1 victory. Both boys bow and shake hands.

The last match is for first and second place. Nick uses a variety of techniques. Near the end he launches a round kick just as the other boy lifts his leg up. Shins collide with a thud.

The match is over, and Nick's opponent limps back to the sideline. The doctor is called over. Nick goes over to console him, not realizing he has just won the first-place gold!

By 4 P.M. Nick is tired. His hip bothers him from the first sparring match, and a jammed finger needs to be iced.

Georganna takes him home. They stop at a Roy Rogers restaurant on the way, and Nick devours two bacon cheeseburgers and a big Chicken Deluxe. Two major victories on three bagels' worth of energy is pretty impressive.

Nick is happy the whole school did well. The Wind Warriors won fourteen medals.

Back home, he hangs his two gold medals on his bedroom wall.

A Surprise

Nick and Sensei kneel face-to-face at the Chatham Dojo.

"You did exceptionally well in the tournament, Nick. Your karate skills have greatly improved. You should be very proud of yourself and your accomplishments. I am promoting you to the rank of *nikyu*, second-degree brown belt," Sensei says. "*Rei*." They bow to each other. "Turn to the class. *Rei*." Nick bows to thank the class for helping him get this promotion.

Nick is promoted on July 11. Now he may wear a thick black stripe around his belt tabs, indicating that he is nearing the black-belt expert rank.

Line Up!

At the Y, Nick directs a young group of yellow belts through the *seisan* kata.

"Turn, punch . . . punch . . . kick . . . punch. David, keep your wrist straight. Get your kicks higher." Their legs snap. Small, clenched fists bite the air.

Waist-high David eyes Nick's brown belt. "I want to be like you some day," he says.

"David, concentrate on your moves. Get your hands up. Now step . . . hook, block . . . hit . . . pull . . . faster, harder!"

He stands like Sensei and tries to appear stern, shouting in a deeper voice. But they all see the smile on his face.

How to Choose A Martial Arts School, Style, or Teacher:

A Note to Parents and Readers

With an estimated 17,000 schools, clubs, and courses in the United States and well over one hundred different styles, choosing the best martial arts school, style, and teacher can be a difficult task. Here are some simple guidelines and ideas to follow.

The most popular martial arts today are karate, tae kwon do, aikido, kung fu wu shu, judo, tai chi chuan, ninjitsu, and jujitsu. No style is the "best." All vary widely in both method of instruction and expression of movement. Start by checking your local library or bookstore for books on these arts to acquaint yourself with their differences.

After you have selected a martial art, the best place to begin looking for a school is in your telephone directory under the general heading "Karate," which should also list other martial arts instruction. In addition to private schools, there are also many fine courses offered by YMCAs, local health clubs, adult schools, after-school programs, dance schools, civic centers, and colleges with classes open to the public. Make arrangements to visit several schools. Look for a clean, well-lit, spacious training area with a suitable place to change into your uniform and class sizes of ten to twenty students.

The most common reasons people pick a particular martial arts school are the following: convenience—it's close to home or work; affordability—the cost is within your budget; good reputation—the program offers what you want and the teacher(s) are experienced; and familiarity—someone you know who is already involved helps you to find out what it's all about.

When meeting with an instructor, ask about his or her background, rank, reputation, years in business, teaching experience, class schedule, number of students per class, types of programs offered, and all the short- and long-term costs of training. If inquiring for your child, ask what experience the teacher has with young adults. Observe at least one class in progress.

A martial art can be an exciting, rewarding activity. Choosing the right school will ensure the best quality of instruction and help you reach your goals.

796.81
Goe

12,630

Community Unit Schools
Dist. #11
Jr. H.S. Library
Hoopeston, Illinois